JAKE AND HONEYBUNCH GO TO HEAVEN

MARGOT ZEMACH

FARRAR STRAUS & GIROUX · NEW YORK

For Mertis and Dan

Copyright © 1982 by Margot Zemach
All rights reserved
Library of Congress catalog card number: 82-71752
Published simultaneously in Canada
by McGraw-Hill Ryerson Ltd., Toronto
Color separations by Offset Separations Corp.
Printed in the United States of America by Rae Publishing Company
Bound by A. Horowitz and Sons
Designed by Atha Tehon
First edition, 1982

JAKE lived just down the road from a town called Hard Times. His only companion was a crazy mule named Honeybunch. Some folks said Jake got Honeybunch from a witch. Other folks said the Devil put a curse on Honeybunch when she ran under a clothesline between Christmas and New Year's.

One way or another, Honeybunch was the most contrary mule that ever lived. Jake couldn't do a thing with her. He used to say: "This misbegotten mule will be the death of me someday!"

So no one was surprised when that day came.

It happened like this. One summer evening the slow freight was chugging through town just as Jake and Honeybunch were crossing the railroad tracks. Now, that train was slow, but Honeybunch was slower. She was taking her own sweet time.

"Get a move on, you devil!" Jake said. Those were the last words he ever said in this world.

It took Jake fifteen minutes to get to the top of the sky and another ten minutes to flip-flop his way along the Glory Road. At last he was in sight of the Pearly Gates.

"Hallelujah!" he hollered. "Here's old Jake come from Hard Times, just been hit by the slow freight." He rang the bell and waited a while, but God's angels were singing and making a powerful sound. "Maybe St. Peter can't hear me," Jake thought. He rang the bell again.

Still no one answered, so he gave the Pearly Gates a little shake. They opened wide enough to let him squeeze through and Jake walked right into Heaven.

There were angels everywhere, and all of them had golden wings. Some extra wings were hanging up to dry. Jake picked out two of the shiniest and tried them on.

As it happened, they were two left wings, but they felt just fine. So Jake took off!

He tried the right-wing dive and the left-wing dip. God's angels were yelling "Be careful" and "Cut that out." But Jake said, "I can't stop now. I'm just a flying fool!"

He picked up speed and did a loop-the-loop. He flew all over Heaven, until finally he got caught in a Heavenly tree, his wings all bent and broken.

Then some of God's angels came and took him over to where God was sitting.

"Jake!" God said. "Who let you into Heaven and where did you get those wings? Couldn't you wait for St. Peter? Go on now, get out of here—and I don't want to see you hanging around the top step!"

"Well," Jake thought, "I never was lucky. Why start now?" Then St. Peter marched him out through the Pearly Gates and slammed them shut.

You never saw a sadder man. "I can't believe it," Jake said. "Now I've lost my only chance to fly around Heaven forevermore."

Just then he heard a familiar sound. *Clippa-clip-clop, clippa-clip-clop* . . . It was Honeybunch, coming along the Glory Road. "Whoaa there," Jake told her. But Honeybunch paid no attention. She went right up and banged on the Pearly Gates.

As soon as St. Peter came out, Honeybunch saw the Great Green Pastures of Heaven. She let out a holler and charged straight inside. "Well," Jake said to himself, "she won't last long."

Honeybunch went rampaging all over Heaven. She was so excited that she rolled in the clouds, kicking and carrying on, scattering angels in every direction.

"That sure is one jumpy mule," God said. Some of his angels tried to catch Honeybunch, but they couldn't even get near her. So God said to St. Peter: "All right, go get Jake. Tell him to come and catch his crazy mule."

Jake was still sitting on the top step, listening to all the fuss. "I'm on my way," he shouted when he heard St. Peter call his name. He came running and grabbed hold of Honeybunch as best he could.

"Stop this ruckus, you crazy mule," Jake said in her ear, "or you'll never get a chance to graze in those Green Pastures. You'll be out on the top step just like me." When Honeybunch heard that, she put her ears down and got real quiet.

After all the angels calmed down, God spoke. "Jake, I appreciate your help with that mule, and so I'm going to give you one more chance. I need a Moon Regulator to hang the moon out at night and put all the stars in their places. If you do a good job, I'll see that you get a pair of wings."

"Lord, I'm your man!" Jake said. And he ran to hitch Honeybunch to the Moon Regulator wagon before God could change his mind.

The wagon was already loaded with stars, so they set off across Heaven, with Jake rolling the moon along.

And every night after that, Jake and Honeybunch went out to hang up the moon and the stars.

Then when morning came, they collected them all again. Jake never forgot even a single star.

After a while, God had Jake fitted up with a beautiful pair of wings, just the way He promised.

So if you don't see the moon and the stars shining some night, it's because Jake and Honeybunch are taking a little time off. You can bet that Honeybunch is grazing in those Great Green Pastures and Jake is loop-the-looping all over Heaven, just like a flying fool.